PIRATES of the CARIBBEAN
THE CURSE OF THE BLACK PEARL

A Pirate's Life

Adapted by Tennant Redbank
Based on the screenplay written by Ted Elliott & Terry Rossio and
Screen story by Ted Elliott & Terry Rossio
and Stuart Beattie and Jay Wolpert
Based on Walt Disney's *Pirates of the Caribbean*
Produced by Jerry Bruckheimer
Directed by Gore Verbinski

Printed in United States of America
First Edition
1 3 5 7 9 10 8 6 4 2
Library of Congress Catalog Card Number: 2006909028
ISBN-13: 978-1-4231-0732-3
ISBN-10: 1-4231-0732-2

DISNEY PRESS
New York

Chapter 1

Gray fog covered the ocean. A tall ship cut through the gloom. At the front stood Elizabeth Swann, the daughter of the governor.

All of a sudden, Elizabeth spotted something in the water. "Look! A boy!" she shouted.

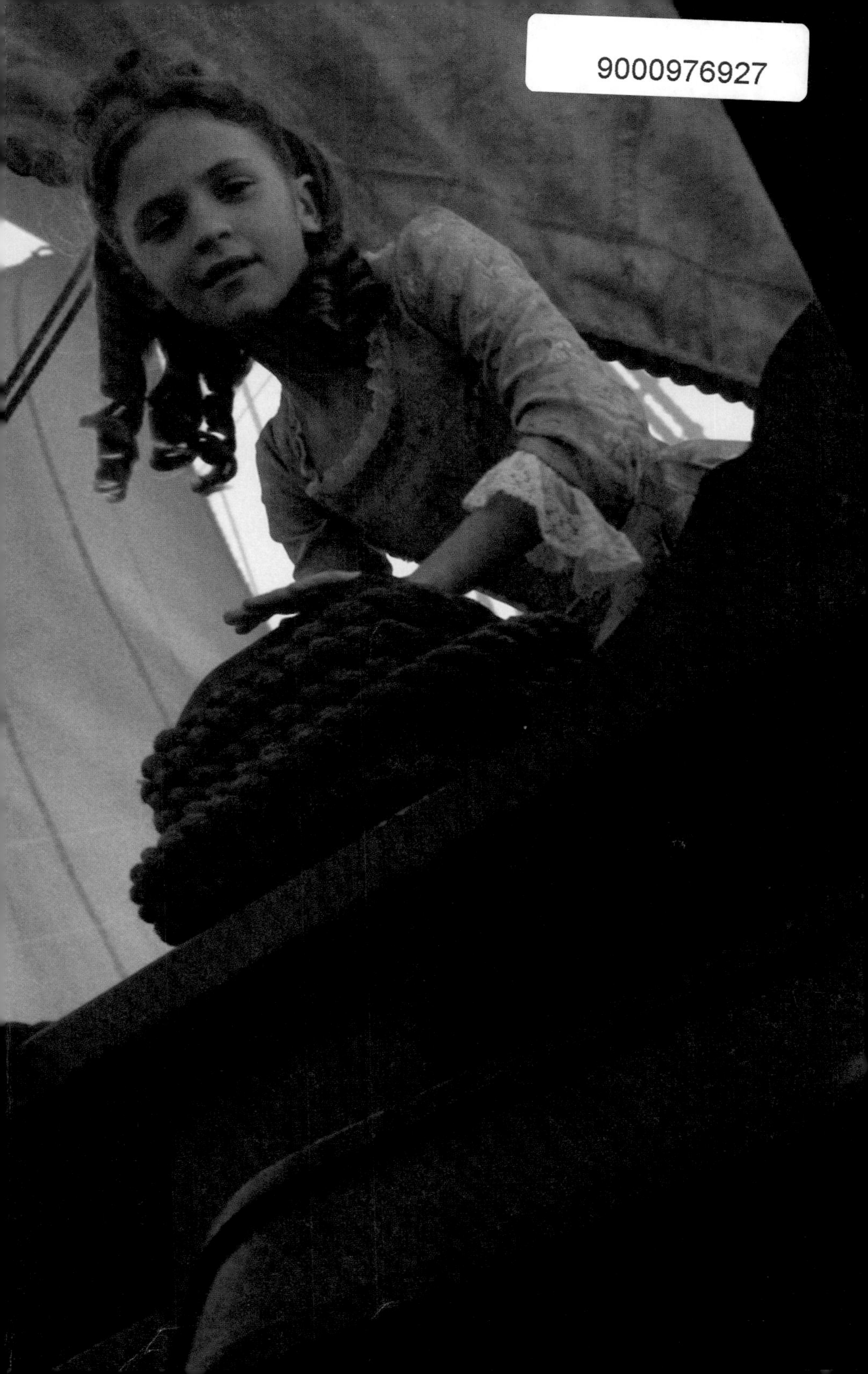

Sailors pulled the boy onto the ship. Elizabeth stood next to him.

Around his neck was a medallion. Elizabeth gasped. She knew what the skull on it meant. "You're a pirate," she whispered. She took the Medallion off his neck and put it around her own. She had to protect him.

Eight years later, Elizabeth was a lady.
And the boy, Will Turner, was a blacksmith.
Ever since the day Elizabeth found him,
Will had been in love with her. But she
was to marry Commodore Norrington of
the Royal Navy.

Even so, Elizabeth cared for Will. She
still secretly wore his Medallion. She didn't
know it would bring her trouble. Already
its gold was calling to a band of pirates,
bringing them to Port Royal!

The pirates sailed in a ship with black
sails and a skull-and-crossbones flag.
The ship was called the *Black Pearl*. And
all the men on it were cursed. They were
searching for the Aztec Gold that had
put the curse on them.

Late at night, the pirates came for the
gold. The *Black Pearl*'s cannons fired at
the fort. Pirates swarmed the streets.
Two found their way to Elizabeth's room.

"We know you're here, poppet," one of the pirates whispered.

"The gold calls to us," the other said.

Elizabeth shivered. She touched the Medallion around her neck. There was nowhere to go.

"Parley!" she shouted. Parley was part of the code of the pirates. It meant the men couldn't hurt her. And they had to take her to their captain.

Through the smoke, Will saw the pirates drag Elizabeth away. He had to save her!

There was one man who could help him. Will ran to the jail. Inside was Jack Sparrow. Once, Jack had been the captain of the *Black Pearl*. But his ship had been taken from him.

"What's your name?" Jack asked Will.

"Will Turner," he replied.

On hearing the name, Jack became thoughtful. He struck a deal. Will would spring Jack from jail. Jack would lead Will to the *Black Pearl*—and to Elizabeth.

Chapter 2

On the deck of the *Black Pearl*, Elizabeth came face-to-face with the new captain, Barbossa. His clothes were made of silk. His teeth were silver and gold. On his shoulder was a ragged monkey.

"I want you to leave," Elizabeth said.

Barbossa wasn't ready to sail away from Port Royal. "No," he answered.

"Very well," Elizabeth said. She darted to the rail of the ship and held the Medallion over the side. "I'll drop it." She knew the pirates wanted this piece of gold. She just didn't know why.

"No!" Barbossa shouted. After a minute, he went on. "What's your name, missy?"

"Elizabeth—" she paused. She didn't think she should give her real name. "Elizabeth Turner," she told him.

With that, Elizabeth and Barbossa made their own deal. The ship turned away from Port Royal. It set a course for the Island of the Dead.

That night, Elizabeth had dinner with Barbossa in his cabin. On the table were trays of food and wine. Elizabeth started eating hungrily. Barbossa just watched.

"Try the wine," he said. "And the apples."

Elizabeth stopped in midbite. The captain was staring at her in an odd way. "You eat it," she said.

"Would that I could," he replied.

Then Barbossa told her a strange tale. Years ago, the pirates of the *Black Pearl* had found a treasure—882 pieces of Aztec Gold. But the treasure was cursed. Every man who took a coin became like a dead man. They couldn't eat or drink or feel. And they couldn't be killed.

There was only one way to end the

curse. The pirates had to bring back all the pieces of gold and wash each in the blood of the man who took it.

"Thanks to you, we have the final piece," Barbossa said. He held up the Medallion.

"And the blood to be repaid?" she asked.

"That's why there's no sense in killing you," Barbossa said. "Yet."

Elizabeth jumped out of her chair.
She ran out the cabin door. On the deck,
the crew was at work. But where the
moonlight fell on them, the Aztec Curse
showed its power. The pirates were, one
and all, skeletons!

Suddenly, Barbossa grabbed Elizabeth.
In the moonlight, his face became a skull.
"You'd best start believing in ghost stories,
Miss Turner," he said. "You're in one."

Chapter 3

Jack and Will were not far behind. They had stolen a ship and followed the *Black Pearl*. The Island of the Dead was where Barbossa had found the treasure. It was where he had to go to end the curse.

Barbossa dragged Elizabeth into a cave. The space glowed with jewels, silks, silver, and gold. In the center was a stone chest.

"Our torment is near an end!" Barbossa cried. The chest was flung open. It was full of gold coins. Each one was marked by a skull.

On top lay a sharp knife. Barbossa picked it up and pulled Elizabeth close to him.

At the cave opening, Will jumped to his feet. But Jack held him back. Now was not the right moment.

"Whose blood must yet be paid?" Barbossa shouted.

"Hers!" the pirates yelled.

Elizabeth shut her eyes and turned her head away. Barbossa cut a red gash across her palm. Then he wrapped her hand around the Medallion.

"That's it?" Elizabeth asked.

Barbossa dropped the Medallion into the chest. The pirates waited. They looked at themselves. They looked at each other. Nothing happened.

"It didn't work!" one pirate wailed. "The curse is still upon us."

"Was your father William Turner?" Barbossa asked Elizabeth.

"No," she said.

The pirates cried out. They began to fight with each other. Elizabeth and the Medallion were forgotten. Suddenly a hand clamped across her mouth. It was Will! Together they slipped away, while Jack stayed to take care of some business with Barbossa.

After a few minutes, the pirates stopped fighting. But Elizabeth was gone. And she had taken the Medallion with her!

"The Medallion! Fetch it back!" Barbossa ordered.

Back on their boat, Will wrapped
Elizabeth's hand with a bandage. "You gave
Barbossa my name as yours," he said. "Why?"

"I don't know," Elizabeth replied. She
pulled the Medallion out of her dress.
"This is yours."

Will stared at the Medallion. "It wasn't
your blood they needed," he said slowly.
"It was my father's blood. My blood."

Will took the Medallion. His father was a pirate. And lately Will had been acting like a pirate, too. He had stolen a ship with Jack. He had sailed with a pirate crew. Will had a lot to think about.

Will and Elizabeth didn't have much of a head start. The *Black Pearl* soon caught up with them.

"We have to fight!" Will cried.

During the battle, Barbossa's monkey scampered onto Will and Elizabeth's ship. It found what it was looking for—the Medallion!

Elizabeth tried to get to Will. But two of Barbossa's pirates grabbed her. They took her onto the *Black Pearl*.

Seeing Elizabeth's capture, Will climbed onto the rail of the *Black Pearl*.

"Barbossa!" Will yelled. He held a pistol in one hand. "She goes free!"

"You've got one shot," Barbossa pointed out. "And we can't die."

"You can't," Will said. "I can." He put the pistol under his chin. Will knew he was no good to Barbossa dead.

"Who are you, boy?" Barbossa asked.

"My name is Will Turner," Will said.

Now Barbossa understood. He agreed to let Elizabeth and Jack go free. And Will would return to the Island of the Dead with him—to break the curse.

Chapter 4

Torches held high, the pirates led Will to the cave. Will's hands were tied behind his back.

All of a sudden, Jack Sparrow strolled into the cave.

"Jack!" Will cried. "Where's Elizabeth?"

"She's safe," Jack told him.

Then Jack explained to Barbossa that Norrington's ship was waiting for him just off the island. Jack thought Barbossa should wait to break the curse. The curse was good for one thing—the pirates could not be killed. Barbossa should use the curse to fight Norrington's soldiers, then break the curse.

Barbossa nodded. He sent his pirates to attack. Still he was puzzled. "Jack, I thought I had you figured," he said. "But turns out you're a hard man to predict."

"Me?" Jack shook his head. Then with his foot, Jack flipped a sword straight into Will's bound hands. "Use it well," he said.

Will did. In a few seconds his hands were free. He turned to fight the pirates who had stayed behind, while Jack battled Barbossa.

Will fought bravely. But he was outnumbered. He fell to the ground. One of the pirates raised his sword.

From out of nowhere, another person knocked the pirate to the ground.

Will couldn't believe it. "Elizabeth?"

Elizabeth grinned at him. Together, they took on the rest of the pirates.

Will was watching Jack closely as well. When the time was right, Will dashed to the chest. He sliced open his hand and grabbed the Medallion with his fist.

Seconds later, a shot rang out. Jack had fired his pistol at Barbossa.

Barbossa looked down at the blood on his shirt. Slowly he understood. The curse had been lifted. He felt angry. He felt shocked. And part of him felt relieved.

"I feel . . ." Barbossa said, ". . . cold." He fell to the ground, dead.

Chapter 5

Back at Port Royal, Jack faced the hangman. Drums beat slowly. Jack's head was put through the noose. The trapdoor opened. Jack dropped. But then a sword flew through the air and stuck into the post. It was Will's sword, perfectly thrown!

Jack's feet found the sword. He balanced on it until he was cut free.

Together, Will and Jack fought
Norrington's men. But there were too many
of them. Soon Will and Jack were cornered!

Norrington walked up to them.
Elizabeth's father was with him.

"You forget your place, Turner,"
Norrington said.

"It's right here, between you and Jack,"
Will replied.

Elizabeth stepped up next to Will. "As is mine," she said.

Norrington was upset. He loved Elizabeth, too. "This is where your heart truly lies?" he asked her.

"It is," Elizabeth told him.

Jack jumped to the fort walls. Before anyone could stop him, he dove into the water. The *Black Pearl* sailed to meet him.

Elizabeth and Will drew together. Elizabeth's father watched them. "You're certain, then?" he asked Elizabeth. "He *is* a blacksmith. . . ."

"No," Elizabeth said. "He's a pirate."

Will smiled. He and Elizabeth turned toward the sea and watched as Jack and the *Pearl* sailed away.